Dedicated to **Chayse and Roman**.

"Silverback and Son" is dedicated to my amazing wife and children who continuously inspire me to be, not only a better father but a better person. This book is based on actual conversations that my son, Roman, and I have had, which means, if you haven't figured it out yet, I'm a gorilla.

Please visit **www.silverbackandson.com** for more information.

"If you could be anything in the whole wide world when you grow up, what would you be?"

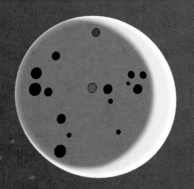

"An ASTRONAUT!"

"So I can float around in outer space."

"That sounds out of this world,"
said Silverback.

"Oh! Oh! I know! I can be a

RACE CAR DRIVER!

I'll drive super fast and win the race."

"I'll be your first customer," said Silverback.

"Well that's a very noble profession," said Silverback.

"Maybe I'll be a
COWBOY!
I can ride around the jungle
on my trusty steed."

"Umm, trusty steed?"
asked Silverback.

"Well your grandfather was a police officer and that's a great job," said Silverback.

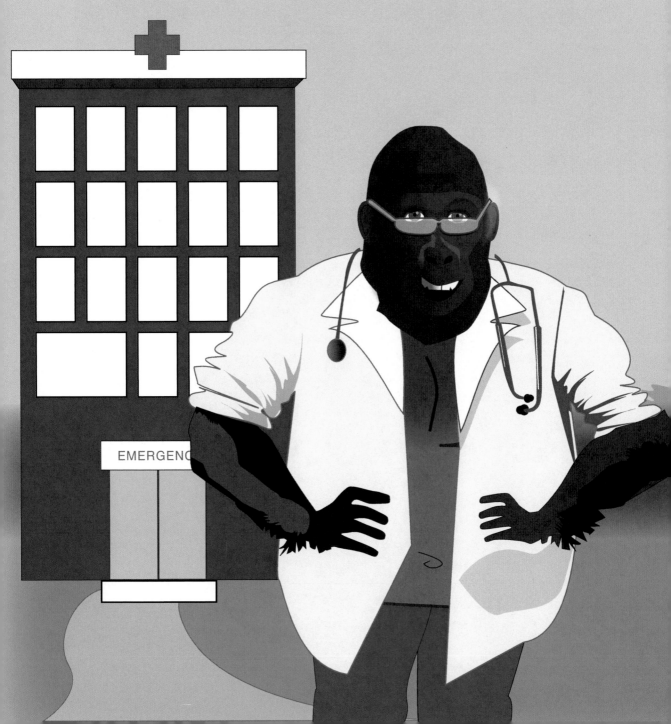

"Well that's very caring of you," Silverback said.

"What do you want to be **MOST** of all?" Silverback asked.

"Most of all?"

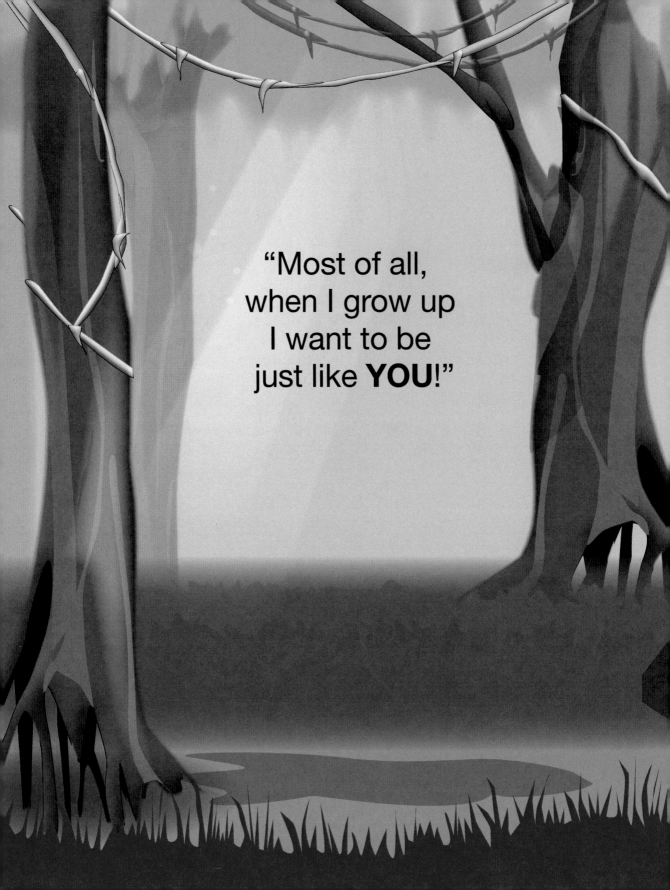

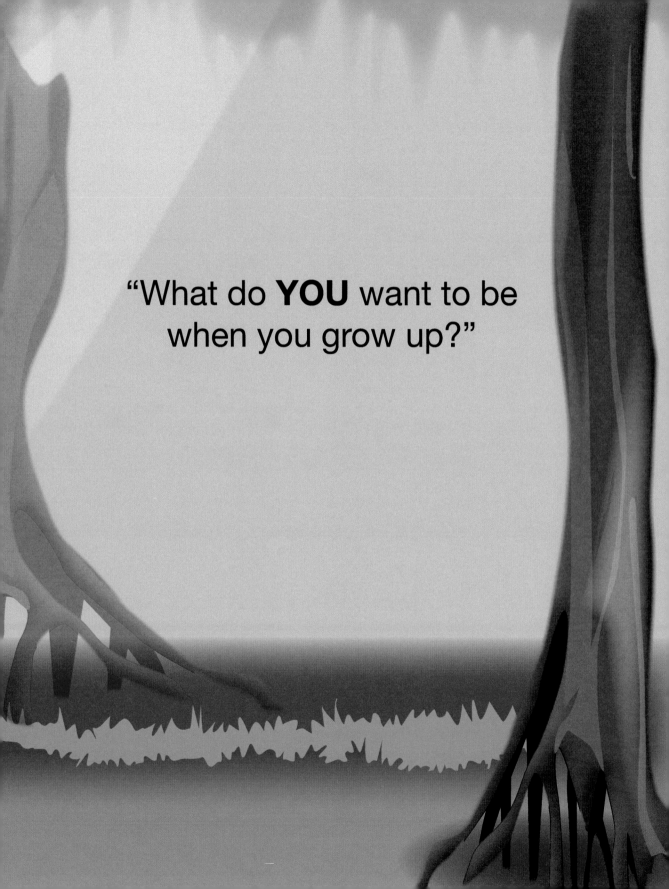

"What do **YOU** want to be when you grow up?"

Made in the USA
Middletown, DE
31 August 2020